'WELL-LOVED TALES'

A LADYBIRD 'EASY READING' BOOK

The Enormous Turnip

retold by VERA SOUTHGATE, M.A., B.Com.

with illustrations by ROBERT LUMLEY

Ladybird Books Ltd Loughborough

Once upon a time,

in the spring,

an old man

sowed some rows of turnip seeds

in his garden.

0 7214 0267 4

As time went by,

the rain fell on the seeds

and the sun shone down on them,

and the turnips

began to grow.

One, two, three, four
(tree bells) it tomb

Every day,

the turnips grew

a little bigger.

But one of them grew much faster

than all the others.

It grew large,

then very large,

then huge,

until at last it was enormous!

No-one had ever seen

such an enormous turnip.

One day,

the old man fancied

a plateful of turnip

for his dinner.

He took off his jacket,

put on his big boots

and went out into his garden.

He gathered up the leaves

of the enormous turnip

in his two hands,

in the proper way,

and he pulled.

He pulled and pulled

with all his might,

but he could not pull up

the enormous turnip.

So the old man called

to his wife

wife
to come and help to pull up

this
the enormous turnip.

The old woman put her arms

around her husband's waist.

Then the old man pulled

and the old woman pulled.

They pulled and pulled

with all their might,

but they could not pull up

the enormous turnip.

So the old woman called

to a little boy

to come and help pull up

the enormous turnip.

The little boy took hold

of the old woman's waist.

Then the old man pulled

and the old woman pulled

and the little boy pulled.

They pulled and pulled

with all their might,

but they could not pull up

the enormous turnip.

So the little boy called

to a little girl

to come and help to pull up

the enormous turnip.

The little girl took hold

of the little boy's jersey.

Then the old man pulled

and the old woman pulled

and the little boy pulled

and the little girl pulled.

They pulled and pulled

with all their might,

but they could not pull up

the enormous turnip.

So the little girl called

to a big dog

to come and help to pull up

the enormous turnip.

The big dog took hold

of the little girl's skirt.

Then the old man pulled

and the old woman pulled

and the little boy pulled

and the little girl pulled

and the big dog pulled.

They pulled and pulled

with all their might,

but they could not pull up

the enormous turnip.

So the big dog called

to a black cat

which means *me*

to come and help to pull up

the enormous turnip.

The black cat took hold

of the big dog's tail.

Then the old man pulled

and the old woman pulled

and the little boy pulled

and the little girl pulled

and the big dog pulled

and the black cat pulled.

They pulled and pulled

with all their might,

but they could not pull up

the enormous turnip.

The black cat called

to a tiny mouse

which means

to come and help to pull up

the enormous turnip.

The tiny mouse took hold

of the black cat's tail.

Then the old man pulled

and the old woman pulled

and the little boy pulled

and the little girl pulled

and the big dog pulled

and the black cat pulled

and the tiny mouse pulled.

They pulled and pulled

with all their might.

And this time

they did pull up

the enormous turnip!

It came up with such a jerk

that they all fell down

flat on their backs.

The enormous turnip fell
  on top of the old man.
The old man fell
  on top of the old woman.
The old woman fell
  on top of the little boy.
The little boy fell
  on top of the little girl.
The little girl fell
  on top of the big dog.
The big dog fell
  on top of the black cat.
The black cat fell
  on top of the tiny mouse.

After a moment,

they all jumped up,

shook themselves

and started to laugh.

They laughed and laughed

for a long, long time.

Then they carried

the enormous turnip

into the old woman's kitchen.

The old woman

cut up the turnip

and cooked it for dinner.

Then the old man

and the old woman

and the little boy

and the little girl

and the big dog

and the black cat

and the tiny mouse

all had turnip for dinner.

They all ate and ate

until they were full.

But they could not eat all

of the enormous turnip.

There was plenty of it left

for dinner the next day

and the day after.

And that was the end

of the enormous turnip.

Series 606D
A Ladybird Easy-Reading Book